About the Book

Shadow was bewildered. He could not understand why his mate, Silver, would not let him enter their den. Finally after fourteen days, she allowed him in to see his first offspring, six newborn wolf cubs.

From the beginning, each cub has a distinct personality. As they develop, their individual traits grow even stronger. Dawn is playful, Blondie serious, Dusky timid. Blackie and Tundra, both strong, intelligent males, show qualities that could make one of them the leader of a pack.

During summer days spent in play, the cubs learn many of the things they will need to face their first Arctic winter. The adults, Silver, Shadow, and Old Two Toes, are never far away. They share in the responsibility of feeding, protecting, and teaching the cubs in an intelligent, flexible manner that reflects a knowledge of the world based on learned experiences. Their treatment of the cubs clearly shows a strong sense of family feeling and a mutual respect for each other that belie the ugly myths that have developed about the wolf as a killer to be feared and exterminated. In a large part, the cubs' survival depends on their ability to withstand attack from human, as well as animal, enemies.

Michael Fox, in his fascinating and authoritative narrative, helps us understand the part the wolf plays in the preservation of the balance of nature and wilderness areas. True-to-life authentic drawings by Charles Fracé show the wolf in his natural environment and enhance our appreciation of a magnificent animal of the wild.

THE WOLF

by Dr. Michael Fox

Illustrated by Charles Fracé

Coward, McCann & Geoghegan, Inc.

New York

For my own two cubs,
Wylie and Camilla

Contents

1

Children from the Earth

It was early may, and the misty air was filled with earth smells drawn out by the rising sun. Shadow, a five-year-old wolf from the Alaskan Brooks Range, paced anxiously in front of the den. He was waiting for Silver, his three-year-old mate, to come out to join him and Old Uncle Two Toes, for it was time to go hunting. He put his head into the entrance and gave a low whine, but she did not reply.

Silver had spent much of the previous night clearing out the old den that her ancestors had used for generations. It overlooked a long valley, and from there herds of caribou and single stragglers could be spotted over a mile away.

Shadow nervously scratched himself, rooted his nose into the mound of soft earth at the mouth of the den, shook his head, sneezed, and then cautiously crawled down into the den. He quickly backed out when a growl from Silver twenty feet away told him to keep away.

Meanwhile, Old Two Toes squatted unperturbed on a lookout knoll a few yards away, snapping at flies and scanning the valley below. He had seen she-wolves behave this way before, and he knew that before the next sunrise, both he and Shadow would have new responsibilities.

Shadow approached Old Two Toes and nuzzled the side of his face affectionately, but suddenly his companion stiffened and gave a low muffled grunt of warning. Shadow looked in the direction of Old Two Toes' gaze, and far below across the valley, he spotted a hunter. Both wolves were ready to slide silently away, staying out of range of the hunter, but keeping him always in sight. Many hunters and trappers say that although they rarely see a wolf, they know that they are being watched, that the eyes of the wolves are on them.

The lone hunter started to climb up from the valley, moving closer and closer to the den site. Shadow gave a low growl-bark that warned Silver of approaching danger. What should he do? He and Old Two Toes should move off to save themselves, but Silver, for some reason, could not or would not come out of the den. The hunter would certainly get her.

Suddenly Old Two Toes disappeared, and seconds later he appeared on a ridge some five hundred yards away from the den and stood there, silhouetted against the morn-

ing sky. The hunter did not see him and continued to climb toward the den. The stillness of the valley was abruptly pierced by a series of staccato barks, ending in a short howl. It was Old Two Toes. He remained on the ridge until the hunter raised his gun at him. The rifle cracked, but Old Two Toes was gone, appearing again for a moment farther along the ridge, downwind from the den. The hunter altered his course and took after Old Two Toes. The wolf had used himself as a living decoy to lure his enemy away from the den. Silver was safe, and Old Two Toes could outwit the most tenacious hunter, even in the depth of winter, when tracks in the soft snow were so easy to follow.

Toward the middle of the afternoon, Shadow, who had been alternately dozing and watching beneath a rocky outcrop below the den site for signs of the hunter, was rallied by a distant howl. Old Two Toes was calling him. The hunter had long since given up on the gray wolf, knowing that he had been fooled by a wily and intelligent animal. Old Two Toes carried with him a constant reminder about hunters. When he was a strong-headed and uncautious one-year-old, his right forepaw had been caught in a trap. To escape, he had had to bite off part of his foot, leaving him with two toes.

Shadow took off in the direction of Old Two Toes' call after he had whined to Silver to come out of the den. But she refused to join him. He left, puzzled by her behavior. He could hear her panting fast and loud, as though she had just run down a caribou in the soft deep snow.

At the fork of the Salmon River, Shadow picked up the scent of Old Two Toes, laid down by the wolf's moist feet, and found him resting half a mile farther downriver. The older wolf got up, briefly wagged his tail, and after they had both brushed faces together in mutual greeting, they took off downriver to eat up the remains of a caribou they had caught the day before.

When they reached the caribou, the two wolves circled the carcass cautiously. When they found no trace of human scent, they knew it was safe to approach the dead caribou. If the frustrated hunter had found it, he might have hidden a trap or even poisoned the meat.

They lay down and began eating when suddenly a dark shadow swooped down and momentarily startled them. It was Hop-a-long, the tattered wise old raven who often trailed the wolves, knowing by their behavior when he might get a meal. He hopped within a yard of Shadow, preened himself nervously, and pecked at nothing between his toes. The wolves ignored him, so he edged closer and shared in the leftovers.

Satisfied and full, the two wolves licked their paws. Shadow bent down and rubbed the side of his face across the torn skin of the caribou. The odor was delicious, and he rolled on his back in ecstasy.

In a flash he was up and lunged at Hop-a-long with his mouth open in a playful expression. The raven cawed, flew up in the air, and then swooped on the wolf, finishing the mock attack by landing in front of Shadow, just out of reach. Shadow lunged again, and the game continued until the old bird grew tired and flew off into a nearby stand of spruce trees.

Shadow, still in a playful mood, bowed in front of Old

Two Toes and then leaped at his shoulder, in mock attack. His uncle turned away, blocking him with a quick twist of the hips. It was time to return to Silver.

The moon was up behind a veil of clouds by the time they reached the den. As the wolves approached the entrance, they could hear muffled groans. Silver was in distress. Had the hunter returned and emptied his rifle into the den? If he had, he had left no tracks or scent.

Abruptly the groaning stopped, and the two wolves heard busy licking sounds and then a noise that made Shadow cock his head to one side and whine in reply. The first moist, mewing dark-brown cub had been born. Even though Silver had never given birth before, she knew instinctively how to care for the cub.

Shadow became excited and curious and started to wriggle down into the den to investigate. Silver whined briefly, telling him she was all right and that she still cared for him, but the growl that followed told him to keep away. Shadow would have to wait fourteen days before he would be able to meet his offspring.

As the night passed, Shadow and Two Toes lay near the den and heard five more bouts of panting, groaning, licking, and mewing. By dawn all was silent, except for the occasional grunt of satisfaction from a warm cub being nursed by Silver and the odd squeal when she moved and accidentally stepped or lay on one of her hungry babies in the cramped hollow of the den. She was the mother of four male and two female cubs.

2

The Hunting Family

ALL SIX CUBS were attached to her teats and were gorging themselves on her rich milk. At intervals Silver would lick their faces, and this would briefly wake them up and make them root into her flank and start sucking again. She also licked their hindquarters and swallowed everything the babies passed. This is an essential part of wolf hygiene. Baby wolves are too young to care for themselves, and they would soon make a mess of the den if their mother did not attend to them. They only pass anything when their mother licks them.

The dew was heavy that morning, and a light breeze

coming up the valley carried the scent of caribou to the wolves. Since the mist had not yet been burned off by the sun, the two male wolves could not use their keen vision to spot caribou. They took off anyway in search of food, descending into the valley in that tireless rhythmic lope that enables wolves to cover vast distances without tiring. They must find food now, with a family to provide for, and work twice as hard since Silver, an expert hunter, would be unable to hunt with them for several days to come. But food was scarce. It had been a long hard winter, and the moose and caribou were few in number and had fewer calves than usual.

Wolf cubs are usually born between April and early May, when there is plenty of food. But when few, if any, sick and old caribou have survived the winter and when the cows are in poor condition and either have no calves or insufficient milk to raise a calf, the wolf family suffers also. Normally there is a fine balance between wolves and their prey. Wolves kill out of necessity, not for the pleasure of killing. A wolf would rather sleep and play, but he must eat. Being a sensible animal, he will not attack a healthy adult. This wastes his energy, or he might be injured, which could stop him from hunting. Usually the wolf only kills sick, aged animals or weak ones. This is actually beneficial to his prey—be they caribou, moose, or deer. Unhealthy animals are not good for a herd because the land cannot support too many nonproductive individuals. They use up the food needed for healthy mothers, their babies, and adult males.

14

Without wolves and other animals to control their numbers, the herd would become too big and could eventually be wiped out by widespread famine.

It is hard to think that a predator—one that kills other animals for food, like the wolf, lion, cheetah, and eagle—performs such a service to the prey that it eats. But this is one of the wonderful relationships that has evolved over hundreds of thousands of years between different animals sharing the same land or habitat. The wolf helps the caribou survive, and the caribou helps the wolf survive. Each does a service to the other in balanced harmony. This balance is easily upset. In many parts of Canada and North America, wolves have been exterminated by ignorant but not always intentionally inhumane or cruel people. Cruelty is often the result of ignorance. It is just as cruel to let herds of deer grow too large so that thousands die of starvation. Man has realized his stupidity and now has to fill in for the wolf by killing off many deer to keep the wild herds at the right number. It is hoped that one day wolves will be allowed to thrive again in the wilderness areas and national parks and that the balance of nature will again be restored.

Sometimes, in the winter, wolves will kill as many caribou as they can at one time—much more than they can eat at one meal. This is necessary because caribou in large numbers are not often seen in winter. Hunters that see this happen think that the wolf is a killer. Yet the Eskimo will kill many caribou and store them in deepfreeze pits in the earth to supply his family through the long winter, and he is not called murderous, but sensible. So is the wolf. The

15

pack will use these kills throughout the winter if they can't get fresh food. The meat soon freezes solid and is safe to eat all winter.

This is what Old Two Toes, Silver, and Shadow had done, but their food supply was all gone, and they had not been very successful in catching fresh food that spring. Now was a crucial time. Would the speed and strength of Shadow and the wisdom and cunning of Old Two Toes be enough to ensure the survival of the trio and the six helpless hungry cubs that seemed to have no end to their appetites?

3

The Threat
of Starvation

THERE WAS NO SIGN of Old Uncle Two Toes or Shadow by
sunrise the next day. Silver was beginning to feel the nag-
ging pains of hunger because she hadn't eaten for three
days. Worse still, her cubs were constantly taking her milk,
and if she did not eat soon, her system would begin to
utilize her own body store of nutriments to keep the milk
supply going. She could not afford this because her body
reserves were low after a long and hard winter. Her milk
would soon become thin and sparse and of little value for
the hungry cubs. One of them began to cry, and no matter
how much she licked it and fussed over it and guided it

17

with her nose toward her nipples, it kept crying. All the cubs were restless and were beginning to compete for the two teats near her groin which produced the most milk. But the supply was running low.

Silver crawled out of the den into the warm morning light and moved silently down the hill to a small spring, where she quenched her thirst. This would at least ease the hunger contractions of her stomach for a little while. On the way back to the den she rooted under some stones and earth where weeks before they had hidden some food, but they had eaten every morsel except for a piece of caribou hoof that smelled of fox. Rastus, the wily red fox, who was always poaching and scavenging from the wolves, had checked this store and had left his scent mark of urine and droppings by their empty larder. Silver sneezed at the strong musky odor of the fox's scent and returned to the den.

The cubs were silent when she entered the den. They had all formed a tight pile by each one wriggling over or under another. Young cubs do this instinctively to conserve heat. For the first two to three weeks of life they cannot maintain their own body temperature by themselves. Silver hesitated about disturbing them—peace at last. But the sickly cub was silent, and she wanted to find out how it was doing. This baby was the smallest and weakest of the litter, and if Silver had been able to get more food during her pregnancy, this cub might have been in better shape. But as it was, the infant was unable to nurse, had crawled into one corner of the nest chamber of the den, and was stiff and cold. It would soon be dead.

18

Silver gently nuzzled and licked it, but the cub merely extended its forelegs and gasped. Slowly it was fading away. One of the cubs in the pile woke up and started rooting around, trying to suck on the ear of one of its litter-mates. Soon the whole pile was awake and moving, and Silver put her head into the squirming mass and gently licked each cub.

A faint whine at the entrance of the den made her stop.

It was Shadow and Old Two Toes. Had they found food? Silver stuck her head out, and Shadow seized her muzzle in his jaws in affectionate greeting. She pulled away and kissed the corner of his mouth and began licking furiously when she smelled that Shadow had been eating.

Suddenly Shadow backed off, lowered his head, gave a great heave, and, throwing up, deposited several pieces of fresh caribou meat at Silver's feet. Their hunt had been successful, and Shadow was performing the age-old ritual of regurgitating food for his mate. Wolves will also do this for injured companions that have to rest and are unable to join them on the hunt for a few days. Silver wagged her tail and, after a short soft howl of pleasure, twisted around and went back to her babies. They would soon have milk. Old Two Toes followed her part way down the corridor of the den, and before Silver could growl-whine and politely ask him to leave, he also regurgitated an enormous heap of meat for her. Some of this he took back himself and then withdrew, leaving Silver with more than enough food for the night.

Over the next few days, the two wolves continued to provide for Silver. Her rich and plentiful milk supply and the plump contented cubs were evidence of their hunting success. Still, the sickly "runt" cub did not revive. Silver found it the morning after the first lifesaving feast. It was cold and still and did not move when she licked it or pushed it with her nose. To Silver, it was no longer a cub, but something that must be removed to keep the den clean. Just as she instinctively ate the membrane sacks in which the cubs were born, so she quickly and efficiently swallowed the lifeless form of her cub.

20

4

Growing Up

AT LEAST ONCE each day Shadow cautiously entered the den, eager and curious to see what the new sounds and smells were that took up so much of Silver's time. But each day he was turned away, until one morning when the cubs were about two weeks old. Silver was lying on her side with her back against the far wall of the den. The five cubs were lined up between her fore and hind legs, each one attached to a teat and alternately sucking, sleeping, and grunting contentedly. She remained quietly on her side and allowed Shadow to crawl down the corridor of the den and enter the large nest chamber where she and the cubs were lying. In the pitch-darkness of the den he found her head and gently brushed it with his muzzle and then licked the side of her face. She returned his affection, and Shadow was at last allowed to meet his offspring. Excitedly, he nuzzled and pawed them, but drew back suddenly when a startled cub squealed. So this is what had kept Silver so preoccupied. Fascinated by the new but vaguely familiar smell, Shadow systematically, and now more carefully, licked each cub, his attentions causing some of them to urinate. Instinctively he cleaned them up.

The cubs were all awake and somehow sensed that something unfamiliar was with them. Their eyes had opened only a couple of days earlier, but the den was dark, and their sight was still poorly developed. Their sense of smell and awareness of soft, warm objects and avoidance of cold had developed quickly after birth. At two weeks old they had learned the smells of the den and could recognize the strong odor of Shadow, a stranger, in the den. Shadow also brought in the cold air of the outside in his fur, and they felt this, too.

One of the cubs rooted hungrily toward him after he touched its head with his nose and then quickly backed away. It crawled after him a little way up the corridor of the den but soon reoriented itself and crawled back to its mother.

The excited Shadow, with curiosity satisfied, left his family and joined Old Two Toes on the lookout knoll to rest up before the next hunt. Both wolves had traveled more than a hundred miles during their last hunt, and they both slept well, lying on their sides with full stomachs and tired limbs stretched out and relaxed.

By three weeks the cubs had grown enormously. Their small ears were beginning to grow straight up, and this, together with their short legs, big paws, and full, round bellies, made them look like fluffy brown teddy bears. Their small oval eyes were no longer cloudy, but slate blue-gray in color. Their baby, or milk teeth, which had begun to come out a week earlier, were now like needles, and Silver was feeling a little sore around her teats, where some of the cubs were beginning to chew and pull instead of sucking.

Little growls and yelps now frequently echoed from inside the den, and Old Two Toes knew that it would not be long before the cubs would be coming out to explore the world and pester him for food and rough-and-tumble play. The cubs were beginning to play with one another by pawing at and licking and chewing one another's faces, necks, and ears. They were also standing and walking a few steps and would even climb over Silver and sometimes chew and pull at her ears and tail. Even the most determined playful attack always resulted in the wobbly cub falling splat onto his chin. When they did bite one another during play, they had to be careful because their sharp teeth could hurt. Within a matter of days all the cubs had "soft mouths" and could control their bites well during playful encounters. They still spent most of their time sleeping and being nursed.

Then, late one morning, one of the cubs managed to crawl up to the entrance of the den. Silver was asleep and didn't notice the curious infant until it was almost too late. A sixth sense told her that something warm, with a familiar smell, was near the entrance of the den. In one fluid move-

ment she was up the den corridor, seized the cub around its chest, and half carried, half dragged it back into the den. A fraction after she had grabbed the cub, a claw raked the earth on the rim of the entrance hole. Talon, the golden eagle, had been waiting for this moment, knowing by the way the wolves had been acting that the den must contain cubs. Silver knew of this danger since one of her brothers had been taken as a cub by the same eagle.

The following evening three of the cubs ventured out
and sat wide-eyed, sniffing at the den entrance with Silver
keeping close guard behind them. All of a sudden the moon
appeared from behind a bank of low clouds. The startled
pups quickly scuttled back inside the entrance of the den.
After a moment, one by one they cautiously peeked out at
the strange thing in the sky.

Shadow and Old Two Toes approached the den, and

Silver came out to greet them. Her high spirits were contagious, and all three greeted each other with much muzzle biting, face licking, and wagging of tails. Silver even rolled over onto her back and remained still while the two wolves sniffed her all over.

There were now five little faces peering out from the den, and Shadow and Old Two Toes went over to look at them. Of the five cubs, Blackie was the biggest; he was bold and headstrong and had to be disciplined the most by the adults. Tundra was the most active of all the cubs. He slept less and explored more than the others and was cautious and seemed to learn things quickly. Dusky was brown-black and the smallest of the three males. Even when a cloud blocked the sun for an instant, he would flatten out and cower or run into the den. It took him a long time to get used to new things and to overcome his fears, and he stood out as the most timid of the litter. The other two cubs were girls. Blondie was an alert and inquisitive cub who often took the initiative and led the other cubs in various activities. Her sister, Dawn, was the most playful of the group. She had a great sense of humor and never took anything seriously. Even when one of the adults was disciplining her, she would try to play and make a game out of it.

When the cubs saw these two seemingly enormous adult wolves, they hesitated at first. Then, one by one, they became excited and began licking and pawing and urinating all over the place. They wiggled on their bellies and wagged their tails so vigorously that they kept rolling and tumbling over one another as they tried to reach up to the wolves' faces. Tundra crawled under Shadow's legs. He stepped gingerly away for fear of treading on the little animal. All three wolves then lay down in front of the den and allowed the cubs to crawl over them. Shadow was watching Blackie straddled across Old Two Toes, trying to chew on his ear, when he was startled by something pulling his tail. Dusky had found a favorite plaything. Dawn started rooting into his side, making loud sucking noises. She was hungry! The disconcerted father stood up, not knowing quite what to do. Clearly, he had much to learn, and to tolerate, in his new role as father and provider. He stood there with his ears back and looked anxiously at Silver, but she was busy grooming herself. When she had finished, she gave a low whine and led the cubs back into the den. Old Two Toes helped by gently pushing one straggler forward with his nose.

The cubs snuggled up beside Silver, too tired to feed, and fell soundly asleep.

5

Uncle Two Toes Takes Over

OLD TWO TOES and Shadow were roused next day by Silver pushing them with her muzzle. She was wide awake and clearly excited about something. She bowed and licked the corner of Shadow's mouth and then seized his jaw affectionately. He raised his tail, growled, and quickly grabbed her muzzle and held her down, showing that he was still boss. He let her go and briefly licked her as Old Two Toes pushed in to pay his respects by nuzzling Shadow's face. Abruptly Silver began to howl in her high-pitched melodious voice. Shadow joined in, followed by Old Two Toe's resonant but somewhat less musical voice. As their chorus climaxed, it was joined by little yelps and howls. The cubs were replying from the dark safety of the den.

Before the birth of the cubs, the three wolves had engaged in this early-morning chorus before they went out hunting. Clearly Silver wanted to get away from the cubs for a while and joined in a hunt. But the cubs could not be left alone. Talon the eagle might appear at any time during the day, and the cubs were not experienced or coordinated enough to get out of danger.

Old Two Toes did a strange thing. He ran up to the lookout knoll over the ridge above the den, down the other side, and lay down in the brush a few yards away from the den. He had taken on the job as baby-sitter, and with their tails high in the air, Silver and Shadow set off to hunt. It had been such a long time since they had been out together that Silver kept prancing ahead and running with her side touching Shadow's flank, like holding hands. They disappeared together over the ridge without even looking back, for they knew the cubs would be safe under Uncle Two Toes' care.

Old Two Toes had been alternating between dozing and scanning for signs of danger for about three hours since Silver and Shadow had gone off hunting. The sun was climbing slowly, and the grass was alive with the sounds of insects busily collecting food and finding companions. His ears pricked, and he looked toward the den when he heard one of the cubs starting to whimper. Soon all five of them were whimpering. When they started to howl and cry mournfully because they missed their mother and were hungry, he got up and went to the entrance of the den. After scanning the hillside and valley below, as well as the sky for the signs of Talon or his mate, he gave a low all-clear whine. The cubs came tumbling out and mobbed him, kissing and pawing his face furiously. They had learned from their mother that a low whine meant "come to me," and she would often reward them by regurgitating a little meat for them. This was the beginning of the gradual weaning process which would be completed by the time the cubs were seven or eight weeks old. They would no longer be dependent on Silver for milk, and she in turn would be able to get herself into condition again, since the hungry cubs had used up much of her body reserves.

Old Two Toes had an empty stomach, and no matter how much the cubs begged, they would get no tidbits from him this morning. He backed off and, baring his teeth, gave a low growl. This surprised and frightened Blondie and Dusky, and they backed off, but the others kept trying to reach his face and lick his mouth. They just didn't seem to get the message. In a flash Old Two Toes turned and seized the nearest cub around the head as though he were going to crush it. The cub struggled and yelped as Old Two Toes held it against the ground until the cub became still. He let go, seized another, pinning it to the ground, and again released it when it stopped struggling. He did this to each cub rapidly, and they were quiet for some time after, even though he affectionately nuzzled their faces and groins after disciplining them. He was teaching them their manners.

This was the first experience for the cubs of being dominated, and they were beginning to learn respect for their

elders. It would not be long before they all knew that a direct stare and a growl meant "keep off" or "don't bother me just now"; otherwise they might be grabbed and pushed to the ground.

The cubs spent much of the day sleeping, playing together, and going in and out of the den. Silver and Shadow arrived before sundown, each depositing an enormous pile of meat near the den after the cubs had heard their whine call and came rushing out to greet them. Old Two Toes was hungry, too, but he waited until the cubs had finished, and then he feasted. The cubs were far from ready for a full diet of solids, and soon all of them were reaching up, trying to seize Silver's full teats. One cub made a mistake and tried to nurse from Old Two Toes and fell over backward in an effort to reach up to the tall wolf. The cubs were still too small to feed while Silver was standing over them, and so she lay down and nursed them in front of the den.

Loud sucking and grunting sounds filled the evening air. But soon silence descended, and the gorged cubs were asleep. Muffled whimpers and yelps came sporadically from the row of cubs against Silver's side, and their little bodies twitched now and again.

6

Wolf Cubs
Have Personalities

DURING THE NEXT few weeks the cubs would spend most of their waking hours learning about one another and the world. Growing up is not easy, and each day a wolf cub is schooled in good manners and taught how to find food and recognize and avoid danger.

Often Old Two Toes watched while the parents went hunting. Sometimes he would go off alone to catch what he could or to eat off Silver and Shadow's kill if it wasn't too far away from the den. Other times he would go off with Shadow while Silver stayed with the cubs.

By four weeks of age the cubs were spending less and less time sleeping and more time exploring around the den area and playing with one another. They could run quite well now. Still, when one cub tried to leap at another during a roughhouse, his front legs would buckle and he would nose-dive or go splat on his chin. Tundra found a caribou leg bone which Shadow had brought back for the cubs a few days earlier. But the cubs were still too young to recognize it as something to play with. He seized one end of it and pulled, dropping it with fright when it made a scraping noise on the earth. Cautiously he advanced again and pawed at it. Gaining confidence, he picked it up and dragged it a few feet. Then he discovered that by holding it in the middle, he could balance it between his jaws and carry it. Proudly, with head and tail up high, Tundra paraded past the other cubs, who were reclining in front of the den. Instantly they chased after him and then fell on their faces as he twisted around to avoid them. When he turned, he clobbered them with each end of the bone. Blackie, one of the bigger cubs, succeeded in grabbing one end of the bone, and Blondie joined in by seizing the other end of the bone when its rightful owner in the middle was distracted. A tug-of-war started, each cub pulling and twisting and growling and yelping. Silver, who was looking after the cubs that day, went over to them, sniffed the bone, and then walked away, deciding that she need not interfere. A parent wolf will often move in among the cubs when they start fighting or playing too rough. Suddenly Blackie, who first tried to steal the bone from Tundra, let go and made a grab for the middle of the bone. This was too much for

Tundra, and he let go and snapped at his brother. Blondie, on the other end of the bone, fell over backward, and the bone rolled down the slope toward Silver. All five cubs ran after it, and since there wasn't a corner or end for all of them, their first fight erupted. Dusky, the smallest male cub, backed off, as did Blondie, while the other three merged into a twisting, rolling ball of growls and yelps. Silver got up and quickly pushed them apart with her nose. The cubs were growing up now and beginning to develop individual personalities, as well as to establish who was leader in the litter.

The day after the incident with the bone, some animosity between Blackie, Blondie, and Tundra, who found the bone first, was evident. They only played together briefly in the morning and kept growling, threatening and pushing at one another. Toward noon, they had a serious fight, which would have a long-lasting effect on the participants. This important fight would settle once and for all who was top cub in the litter. From this time on, even into adulthood, they would know their position or rank. With this knowledge there would be no serious fights for rank when they were older and stronger and so more likely to severely injure one another. Somehow these fights "clear the air" and establish a social order which serves to maintain peace and harmony in the litter.

The fight started when Blondie pushed Blackie roughly with her shoulder after they had been teasing and "testing" each other all morning. It was the last straw for Blackie, and he seized the scruff of Blondie's neck and shook it so violently that he fell over with Blondie now on top of him.

The startled Blondie tried to get away, and accidentally stuck one paw into Blackie's eye. Blackie struck out and drove his sharp canine "fang" teeth deep into poor Blondie's foot. Yelping with pain, Blondie tried to bite anything in reach and, in her panic, bit Tundra on the tail when Tundra, who was watching the fight, got too close. Confused and hurt, Tundra lunged at Blackie, and Blondie limped away to lick her wounds. Meanwhile, Old Two Toes, who was baby-sitter for the day, just stood by and let the cubs settle their differences. He seemed to know, perhaps from past experience, that young cubs have to work things out for themselves.

Tundra and Blackie seemed to be locked in mortal combat. Both cubs had hold of each other's neck scruffs and were wrestling furiously, each trying to throw the other onto the ground. The skin in this area over the shoulder and up the back of the neck and also the cheeks is extremely thick and seems to help reduce the chances of injury since wolves especially attack this area. A kind of inborn rule governs their fighting patterns, and it is only when two rival wolves are really set on killing that they aim at the throat. Fortunately at this age cubs aren't really strong enough to kill each other, and they quickly recover from their injuries.

With a powerful downward twist of his head, Tundra threw Blackie onto his back, but at the same moment, he lost his hold on Blackie's scruff. Blackie held on and fell on top of him. He gave a yelp and let go when Tundra blindly grabbed hold of his ear and then seized him by the cheek and began to shake and shake. Blackie got extremely frightened and began to yelp. All of a sudden Tundra stopped biting and stood stiff and trembling over Blackie. He had suddenly responded to the distress call of Blackie, which "cut off" his attack, and he intuitively understood that he need no longer attack. Blackie sensed this and remained still, but as soon as he moved to get up, Tundra, thinking that he was ready to fight again, growled and snapped at him. Blackie again yelped and lay still. His intentions were then clear to Tundra, who stepped off him and walked away to recuperate. From this time on, the cubs never bit one another during a squabble; they seemed to respect one another's wishes. When Tundra wanted his own way, he only needed to growl and stare at Blackie, who would lower himself, flatten his ears and remain still and even roll over on his side. When Blackie threatened Blondie, she behaved in the same way as Blackie behaved toward Tundra. Often during the following weeks when Tundra put down Blackie by growling and asserting his rank, Blackie would immediately put down Dusky or Blondie if they were close by, even when they were innocently minding their own business.

Dusky and Tundra never had a serious fight and were good friends most of the time, perhaps because Dusky was no threat to Tundra, who was bigger and stronger. The two girls, Dawn and Blondie, both accepted Tundra as the leader of the litter, and between themselves they never had a fight. Blondie, the more serious of the two, always got her own way over Dawn, who didn't seem to care much about anything. She was the playful clown of the group. Yet at times Dawn could be quite crafty. She would bow and pretend to be playful to distract the other cubs when she was intent on stealing their food.

The next four weeks were uneventful. The cubs continued to grow and play and explore the vicinity of the den
area. Shadow, accompanied by either Silver or Old Two
Toes, was very successful in finding food for the family. At
eight weeks of age the cubs lost most of their dark-brown
baby fur, their tails were beginning to get bushy, and their
ears were much bigger. Blackie, however, had one ear that
didn't grow up straight like the other. He probably got this
crumpled ear from the fight with Tundra.

7

A Narrow Escape

LIFE HAD BEEN PEACEFUL and plentiful for the wolves. The cubs were now roaming some distance from the den, although they spent most of the day playing in a small open glade about twenty yards above the den. This glade was littered with their "toys"—an assortment of bones, a large piece of caribou antler, and their favorite toy, a strip of bearskin that Silver had brought back one day after she found a dead bear near the big river. Several paths made by generations of wolves and their cubs led from the glade into the surrounding bushes, where the cubs would shelter from the noonday sun.

One morning a shadow swept silently over the glade. Without even pausing to look up, the cubs scattered into the safe cover of the bushes. They did this instinctively. Even when they were in front of the den, a sudden noise would send them bolting down the hole—they knew exactly where the hole was wherever they were, and when danger came, they could head straight for it. But Dusky, in the middle of the clearing, was frozen with fear. Instead of running for cover, he flattened out and was fixed to the spot. A bark broke the terrible silence, and the cubs saw Silver leap over Dusky, snarling and snapping at the air. Enormous wings beat her face, and a steel claw raked the air inches from her eyes. Talon gave an angry scream and landed a few feet away, his dive at Dusky turned aside at the last moment by Silver. Dusky scuttled away into the bushes as Silver lunged at the eagle, grabbing a mouthful of his tail feathers as he took off. Talon would not return.

It was two days before the cubs would play in the open glade again. From then on, Dusky would always be afraid of being in open areas without cover. Wolf cubs, like dog puppies, never forget an unpleasant incident, especially things that happen in the period around eight weeks of age, and Dusky was permanently scarred by his experience. Because of this experience, Dusky would later help save the lives of the pack by warning them early of danger in the sky.

In this same week, Silver and Shadow had made a kill about a quarter of a mile from the den. This time they did not come back to the den filled with food for the cubs. When the cubs greeted them to be fed, Silver and Shadow jumped over them and ran off a little way. Silver whined, and the cubs came tumbling after her. In this way the two wolves led the cubs away from the den to their first kill, with Old Two Toes trailing behind to encourage a straggler.

As they approached the kill, the carcass of an old caribou with a broken foreleg, the cubs became excited at the smell of food. They ran toward the carcass and abruptly stopped dead. They had never seen food like this before, all covered with fur and with a head, staring eyes, and long legs. The three adult wolves approached and started pulling and tearing at the dead animal. This made its legs move and jerk up into the air. Dusky and Dawn bolted, and Blackie followed them. The terrified cubs peered out of their hiding place behind a nearby bush. Blondie and Tundra did not bolt. They were too fascinated by what the adults were doing. Slowly they crept forward, and Silver looked at them, whined, and wagged her tail to reassure and encourage them. Soon Tundra was tugging at the carcass, trying to tear off a piece of meat, while Blondie, who was so excited that she didn't know whether to play or eat, started pulling the caribou's tail.

One by one the other three cubs came out of hiding and joined the others at the feast. The cubs quickly learned to pull at the meat with their front teeth, using their forefeet to get a good foothold and then to use the back teeth to

chew and cut off pieces. Silver regurgitated some pieces for the hardworking, grateful cubs who weren't getting far the first time by themselves.

Shadow lay down and began crunching up a long bone to get the delicious marrow inside. Splinters of bone and marrow showered Dusky and Tundra, who were struggling with a large piece of meat. Both cubs nibbled up the sweet flakes of marrow, and as soon as the other cubs saw that, they ran over and joined in. A semicircle of cubs formed around Shadow, who continued for some time to break up bones for them. Then Blackie saw Silver walking off with a large steak in her jaws to eat in the shade of a nearby thicket of dwarf spruce trees. He chased after her and grabbed one trailing end of the steak. His mother was hungry, but in the typical good-natured way of a wolf parent, she let go of the meat. Greedy Blackie collapsed under the weight of the meat but valiantly tried to drag it away into a safe corner for himself. Silver bent down to lick at the meat, and Blackie growled and seized her jaw just like an adult who wants to put another wolf down. Silver withdrew, accepting his wishes, but a moment later, the four other cubs were on top of both Blackie and his steak, and a tug-of-war started. One by one the cubs tore off a nice chunk. This was their first lesson in cooperating. Having another cub pull at the other end made it much easier to tear up the meat into pieces small enough for swallowing. Blackie finished up with the biggest piece, and no one challenged him for it. The cubs were beginning to learn to respect one another's property; even the bigger and stronger like Blackie and

Tundra would not bully the smaller ones and force them to give up their goodies.

After the cubs had stuffed themselves, the family trekked home to the den on the hill. The cubs had learned a good deal that day, but they had yet to learn the hardest lesson of all—how to single out, track, and kill their own prey without getting injured or killed themselves.

Back at the den the cubs were thirsty, but Silver refused to allow them to nurse at all. They were now nearly eight weeks old, and she was weaning them seriously. Each time a cub reached up to seize a teat, she jumped over it, turned and snapped, and even pinned persistent Blondie to the ground. Shadow saw what was happening and kept cutting off the cubs by pushing between them and Silver. Silver could have run away to avoid the cubs, but they would only have pestered her when she came back. This way they learned quickly that Silver no longer wanted them to nurse. It was no real hardship since her milk supply was thin, and the cubs got very little when they did feed. Shadow led them down to the spring, and the cubs quenched their thirst, returned to the den to pass out, exhausted and bursting with food.

8

School
and a New Home

DURING THOSE SUNNY WEEKS in the glade, the cubs learned
many things. They added much to their growing list of
odors and could already identify several hundred different
smells and sounds. Their eyes were keener in detecting the
slightest movement in the grass, and they were beginning to
recognize any change in the foliage or earth that a passing
animal might have made. The cubs learned the many
sounds of insects, birds, leaves, grass, and their slow or sudden movements and the smells of earth, flowers, and furry
animals. Everything new was investigated, if possible
played with, and even chewed and tasted.

46

Slowly they learned how to concentrate, how to tune their senses to just one thing and not be distracted by the numerous other things going on around them. They were growing up, and each step was a new experience, a lesson, an investment for the future. Each waking moment was a serious survival lesson, practiced and repeated during play and relived in their sleep. They had much to learn before the winter. By then they had to be self-sufficient. Always one or more of the adults was watching them, encouraging, guiding, protecting, disciplining, caring, feeding and loving. Sometimes they caught small live prey for the cubs, such as baby hares and ground squirrels, for them to practice on. The cubs learned to anticipate the movements of the prey and to counter these movements by blocking and feinting. More than once they were bitten and bleeding before they learned to feint, dodge, and lunge to bite at the right place and at the right moment and avoid being injured themselves. They would limp back to Silver, Shadow, or Old Two Toes, who could console them and tenderly lick their wounds. In a few months they would have to learn how to tackle larger prey—caribou and moose—and these early lessons were a vital start to their continued survival, in a land that was not easy, and where all animals, large and small, would fight to the end to stay alive.

Silver was up first next morning and seemed agitated, pacing to and fro in front of the den. The cubs tumbled out and immediately gave up trying to nurse when she growled and ran over them. Then she took off down the hill, and the cubs tagged along behind, wondering perhaps if they were going to another feast. Shadow and Old Two Toes went on ahead to scout for food.

Soon Silver and the cubs were moving along the bank of the big river when they came up to a rock that fascinated the cubs with its many smells. It was a scent post, one of the many that the wolves marked with their own urine to inform other wolves that might pass of their presence in the area. The cubs would not mark this stone with their urine until they were much older. Silver marked the stone herself after sniffing it and learning that Old Two Toes and Shadow had recently passed by and that the cubs' aunts and uncles from the main pack, whom the cubs had yet to meet, had not been in the area for at least a month.

She led the cubs along for another half hour until they came to a bend in the river. They went onto a sandbar, a length of riverbed that dried up after the spring floods subsided. Here they drank from the river and rested for a while. Silver then walked up the bank and onto a small knoll on the bend of the river. She suddenly disappeared and then reemerged from a large hole concealed under a tangle of tree roots. This was to be the cub's new home, where they would spend most of the summer. The cubs explored, and then Silver showed them a clearing among the willows a little farther up the riverbank. This would be their safe sun-drenched play area and was a place where generations of wolves had left their cubs while they went off to hunt. Food was plentiful in that area in the summer, and the cubs would not have to travel far to feast with their parents.

9

Mr. Grumbly
and Mice Fun

THE CUBS SETTLED DOWN quickly in their new home. That
evening Shadow returned and took them to a kill only a
short way upriver. Before sunset that evening the cubs had
their first face-to-face encounter with an unforgettable
character—Mr. Grumbly, the wolverine.

Tundra was busily exploring the edge of the play area
where a tantalizing new smell was coming from the willows. It was a powerful musky odor that he had never
smelled before. The other cubs, seeing Tundra so excited
and intent on something, loped over to him. But they hung
back behind him, unsure and a little afraid of the powerful

49

smell. They turned tail and bolted when the willows shook and a chattering explosive roar shot Tundra out of the bushes like a rocket. He headed for cover on the far side of the glade, and there the cubs waited, huddled together, shivering with fear and excitement. A small brown form with beady eyes and short stubby legs appeared and leisurely ambled into the center of the glade. Mr. Grumbly was not much bigger than the cubs. Tundra and Blondie edged forward, even more curious. But when Mr. Grumbly stood up on his hind legs and screamed at them with his raucous voice, they scuttled back into the bushes. But they didn't feel safe there, either, since the wolverine, unlike an eagle, had no difficulty plowing through their cover. Actually, Mr. Grumbly wasn't an enemy like the eagle. He just wanted to be left alone, and inquisitive wolf cubs were a nuisance to the old recluse. He realized that these meddlesome cubs were here for the summer, and with a final roar that sent shivers up the cubs, he charged off into the willows and disappeared. His noisy departure was partly intended to impress them, since he was afraid of no one. Even adult wolves had great respect for Mr. Grumbly.

One by one the cubs stepped hesitantly out into the glade and reassured one another by licking, rubbing faces, and wagging their tails. Blondie, who could contain herself no longer, burst into play, running around the others in smaller and smaller circles until she crashed into Dawn. The effect was contagious, and soon the cubs were chasing one another in circles, one trying to grab the tail of another, and then in turn letting others chase it. All four started chasing Blackie, and that was too much for him. He turned, stood his ground, and, bristling all over, snarled and snapped at them. They got the message and broke up into pairs to wrestle with each other, using the same actions that they might have to use as adults in serious combat. But their bites were controlled, and although it looked as though they were going to tear each other apart, no one was ever hurt.

Blackie shook himself and edged off into the bushes. From his hiding place, he eyed his companions, and then crouching low, he stalked them. This was very effective,

since the cubs were so preoccupied with their own game they didn't notice him. They had to learn to stay alert at all times and not get too involved in one thing. Blackie crawled closer, with his body and head close to the ground for concealment and his eyes bright with excitement. Then he charged; his timing was perfect. He seemed to come from nowhere, knocking the cubs over and sending them scurrying for cover. They couldn't believe that it was Blackie, but he repeated the stalking game, lying flat out in the middle of the glade, then suddenly leaping up and charging as each cub came out of hiding. The cubs took to this game fast. Instinctively they were developing the stealth and coordination that would help them stalk and capture food when they were older.

The next morning, while the cubs were playing their new game and Old Two Toes was looking after them, Tundra suddenly froze at one edge of the glade. He was trembling all over, with one paw slightly raised, and his ears thrust forward in complete concentration. The grass in front of him waved slightly and rustled, and he rushed forward, expecting to land on Dawn or Blackie, who were already the best stalkers. But he landed on nothing. Puzzled, he stood still for a moment, cocked his head to one side and leaped sideways to where the rustling sounds were now coming from. Again he caught nothing, and he almost did a somersault when he felt something small run between his legs. He turned around and stabbed the grass with extended forelegs. Under his paws something wiggled, and he pushed his nose down to investigate. The smell was exquisite, and he rolled his chin over it. Suddenly he felt tiny needles piercing his lip, and he shook his head violently. The little field vole let go and went soaring up into the air and landed right in front of Tundra on a bare patch of earth. The dizzy and confused rodent hesitated just long enough for Tundra to trap him under one paw, but from that moment on, Tundra didn't quite know what to do. He wanted to play with the mouse, but some inner urging told him that it was food. He kept the mouse between his paws and was soon surrounded by the other curious cubs. Blackie, with only a moment's hesitation, thrust his head between Tundra's forepaws and grabbed and killed the mouse in one movement. To him the mouse was something to eat rather than something to play with. Taken aback, Tundra growled complainingly and grabbed at the mouse hanging from Blackie's mouth. Blackie, surprised perhaps by the speed and suddenness of his own instinctive prey-killing actions, was slow to react to Tundra, who tore the mouse out of his jaws and promptly swallowed it. They all knew then that mice were good eating, and soon all the cubs were stalking and catching young mice in the glade. A few days later juicy fat grasshoppers appeared and started chirping and leaping in the clumps of long grass in the glade. They provided the cubs with much sport and a tasty treat at the end of the hunting game.

All five cubs were playing with sticks in a clump of willows early one morning when they were suddenly alerted by rustlings, gruntings, and nibblings coming from a dwarf tree a few yards off. They tensed and warily began to stalk, excited by the new odor that came in little bursts on the occasional breeze that played through the trees. They knew that if they rushed, they might scare off whatever it was before they could get close enough to it. Then they saw what it was—a slow, prickle-covered creature that looked at them and didn't seem in the least perturbed. The cubs crouched and waited, and after what seemed a lifetime to them, Lady Amblethorn, a blond and, perhaps to other porcupines, a very beautiful young female, slowly climbed down the tree and started to amble off to eat the bark off another tree. The cubs tensed, ready to give chase, but stopped abruptly when Shadow gave a low warning growl that meant danger. The cubs couldn't understand this, because the porcupines was small, slow, and seemed an easy prey. But they obeyed their father, because by this time they had learned all the signals—the growls, whines, and silent messages of the face, eyes, ears, body, and tail. Not to obey meant a sharp nip or stab in the side or even a shake, followed by being pinned to the ground. The cubs all knew the signals that meant stay, stop, be silent, or come, it's OK, all's clear. Shadow cautioned the cubs again and then called them. They followed him back to the glade.

A few days later they found a dead porcupine and knew something of the dangers when inquisitive noses felt the sharp quills. Shadow had great respect for porcupines. As a yearling, one of his foolhardy but half-starved brothers had tangled with one. He remembered him slowly dying in agony, unable to hunt, and severely infected by quills in his feet, eyes, nose, mouth, and throat. A terrible lesson, which Shadow in part passed on to his children.

54

Thin wispy phantoms of mist drifted across the river, and the dew was heavy on the long grass as the cubs went for their morning drink. All the cubs except Dusky, the most timid of the cubs, had overcome their fear of water, and they plunged in and wallowed in a shallow lagoon. Blondie felt something under her feet, and after two unsuccessful attempts to paw it up, she thrust her head completely under the water and came up with her prize: a long smooth stick, one of her favorite playthings. A light breeze rippled the water, bringing a familiar smell, which immediately alerted the cubs. They turned their faces into the breeze and sniffed and flopped forward in the water, following the scent which got stronger and stronger as they advanced. Dusky, anxious not to miss anything, took the plunge and caught up with his companions, who were now climbing onto a sandbar and still sniffing in the direction of a large clump of willows growing in some shallows at the river's edge. Suddenly all the willows swayed and parted, and the largest moving living thing that they had ever seen emerged. It was so big that at first the cubs couldn't make out what it was. Then the pieces began to fit together—an enormous rump, a long Roman nose, incredible antlers, and long, powerful legs. The cubs huddled together and edged forward, tantalized by the odor of something so enormous, each feeling afraid, but secure in the presence of companions. Dusky nervously licked Tundra's face to reassure himself, and Blackie frightened himself by barking for the first time. He didn't seem to know where the bark came from.

Caesar, the moose, eyed the cubs with curious aloofness, recognizing them as harmless little creatures that were no match for his speed and strength. When a pack of hungry wolves had circled him that winter, Caesar, who was getting on in years, remained cool and calm. If he had run instead of standing still and keeping his ground, they might have killed him. Instead, he had kept the pack at bay with flailing feet, and after three hours, the wolves had left him alone.

Nonchalantly he tore off a willow branch and nibbled at a few leaves while the cubs, huddled together on the sandbank, stared wide-eyed, like curious children. Caesar continued to browse leisurely for a while and then, with more agility than grace, stepped onto the bank and ambled off without so much as a glance at the cubs. Instantly the cubs rushed across the sandbank as though to chase the moose, thinking that they had put him to flight, but their confidence was short-lived. Caesar turned and shook his great antlers to drive away some biting flies from his rump. The cubs took this as a threat, and tumbling over one another, they scrambled back over the sandbank to the lagoon and, with tails between their legs, climbed the bank and raced homeward. Silver, who had been watching all the while from a gravel pit on the riverbank, intercepted the cubs and led them to eat from a recent kill a short distance downriver. The cubs were overjoyed to see her and kept close to her heels all the way instead of running off for a while and catching up later as they usually did. Old Caesar had created a vivid impression on the young wolves!

10

More School—
for Winter

IN A FEW WEEKS the days began to get shorter, and the morning air had a nip to it that would soon turn into frost. By late August the cubs, now nearly five months old, were traveling quite far with one or more of the adults and learning more each day about their home range. They learned where they could find water, even in the driest, hottest summers, and they learned where the best places were to spot and to stalk prey. They also learned the location of two other den sites which had been used the previous year by the main pack. They had not seen Old Two Toes for several days. Perhaps he had gone off and joined the main pack some fifty miles away. This was the month when the cubs would first meet their other relatives and would also join in their first hunt with Silver and Shadow.

About fifteen miles downriver, Silver and Shadow took the cubs onto a lookout knoll that gave them an excellent view of the river valley. It was a crisp, clear day in late August, and caribou were scattered in the valley to browse before the mosquitoes came out and drove them to higher slopes, where the wind kept the insects away. In June and July the mosquitoes were much thicker and, together with the terrible botflies that fill the caribous' nasal passages with their grubs almost to the point of suffocation, were a constant irritation to the poor caribou.

The wolves spotted one caribou that was in poor condition and breathing with difficulty because of the parasites in its nose. It spent more time shaking and pawing its head than grazing. Today the cubs did not stay behind their parents to watch the kill from a safe distance. Silver and Shadow called them to follow. This would be the first encounter with a large prey for the cubs at close quarters. It was dangerous because the caribou could kill a small cub or, worse still, smash a leg or jaw and wound him so that he would die from an infection or starvation. But the cubs had watched how carefully the experienced adults avoided the feet of caribou and moose and how they avoided injury by attacking the flanks and shoulders of their prey. An adult wolf could knock down a small caribou with one rush. The cubs had practiced this and other actions during play with one another, but they were still too small for the real thing. The two adult wolves circled their prey, and the cubs fol-

lowed gingerly. Silver stood up to make herself obvious to
distract the sick caribou while Shadow got behind and
grabbed at its flank. As soon as the caribou turned to fend
off Shadow, Silver rushed forward and struck its shoulder,
knocking it down with the force of her own impact. The
wolves did not kill the caribou instantly, but seemed to be
holding it down for the cubs.

Tundra was the first to approach the struggling caribou, and he cautiously grabbed its tail, a safe place to attack and one where he could get a feeling for the power and unpredictable movements of the prey. The others, except Dusky and Dawn, encouraged by Tundra's success, rushed in, Blackie getting hold of an ear and Blondie trying her strength on the caribou's rump. Dusky and Dawn were still

hesitant, and Dusky kept whining and rushing forward and then back to Dawn. Suddenly the caribou lay motionless. This was the most dangerous moment for the cubs, because the caribou was only shamming death.

Dusky and Dawn edged forward on their bellies but scooted off when the old caribou lashed out with one hind foot. The other cubs had not relaxed and were prepared, if not actually ready for this, because both Silver and Shadow had remained tense and vigilant while the caribou lay motionless. Suddenly Silver bit the caribou several times in the neck, and the sick animal was put out of its misery.

The cubs then became excited when they saw Silver and Shadow relax and start tearing at the soft belly skin of the caribou. Although the meat was tough and stringy, it was the best meat that Tundra, Blondie, and Blackie had ever eaten. The timid cubs, Dawn and Dusky, still had to overcome their fears. This would soon happen with the help of their parents and the encouragement of their own litter-mates.

After the meal, Shadow rolled in the musky odor of the carcass, and some of the cubs followed him, engaging in an age-old social ritual. Then seven heads were lifted to the sky, and they sang out a soft, full-stomach chorus to the mountains.

11

The Cubs
Become Hunters

AFTER MILLIONS OF YEARS of evolution, species of animals, such as rabbits, mice, deer, and caribou, that are used as food by others have had to adapt to survive. One of the ways is by producing a surplus of offspring. Each year the predators—mountain lions, foxes, coyotes, and wolves—use up this surplus, and the main prey population is left unmolested. It is even improved because the sickly young are the first to be killed. If the animals' predators were removed, usually by man, they would still continue to produce a surplus of offspring. The survival of all these offspring would lead to starvation, and the whole population would be wiped out. With land grazed so quickly it cannot regrow fast enough, it would take years for the earth to recover and for the population of a species to build up again.

With a surplus of young prey, what is there to stop wolves from killing too many and increasing their own numbers? The first reason is that the baby moose, deer, and caribou are all born at around the same time, so that wolves can never have repeated orgies on helpless newborn animals. Second, within a few hours, the babies, if they are healthy, can run well and keep up with their mothers. If the wolves ever did overkill or have too many cubs themselves, they would soon deplete their resources and starve to death. Winter is a hard time for wolves, some worse than others. The scarcity of food during a bad winter helps keep the wolf population from getting too big. Many cubs die during their first winter. The relationships between wolves and their prey is complex and is one of the wonders of the balance of nature.

The cubs spent many hours attentively watching the adults hunting. This was high school for them, and not to attend could mean starvation or injury and death. They saw how the wolves used the wind to help locate prey and to conceal their presence by always keeping the wind in their faces. They prey would not then smell the wolves. Every bit of available cover—a rock, a hollow, a bush—was carefully studied and remembered as the direction of stalking and ambush plans were worked out.

They saw and learned how the adults placed themselves and sometimes signaled to position themselves for ambush, for driving game toward a companion, and how they would run the prey in a great circle, each wolf cutting across its path until the prey was exhausted. They saw the adults set herds of caribou running to test them and help pick out the sickly animals. Later they learned to recognize which might be the easiest prey without even running them.

They acquired great knowledge about the behavior of all the animals that they could eat and also of those which were dangerous. Through observation the cubs gained the knowledge necessary for their survival. They were hunters in the true sense—with a knowledge of ecology and behavior, knowing all the relevant details of the life habits of every animal in their domain. The Indians and Eskimos used similar hunting methods. Perhaps they too had learned from the wolves.

12

Reunion

AROUND SUNSET one early September evening, with the last of the migrant ducks winging into the growing darkness, the wolf family was playing in the clearing by the willows. The peace was broken by a long, mournful cry from the distant hills, and then another and another. Shadow and Silver stood up, approached each other, rubbed noses, and then raised their heads and gave a more excited series of short and long howls. They paused and from the hill, closer now, it seemed, their howls were answered. Shadow became very aroused and pranced around with his tail up, and the hair stood straight up across his shoulders. Silver bent down in front of him and licked the side of his face, and he growled and pinned her to the ground. The cubs ran over to their parents, and Shadow growled at them, too, showing that he was master. He was preparing himself and putting his family in line for the coming of his relatives. It was the main pack that called, and he and Silver had told them where they were. Soon the cubs would meet their kin— Grayface, Shadow's mother, Storm, who was father to both Shadow and Silver, and their four offspring from the previous year. Perhaps Old Two Toes might be with them as well.

The night was a sleepless one for the cubs. They were so excited by the change in behavior of Silver and Shadow and by the howls that came closer and closer and that Silver and Shadow occasionally answered.

At dawn they saw the main pack coming in single file along the riverbed, avoiding the deep water by jumping from one sand or gravel bar to another. Storm was in the lead, followed by Grayface and two large black wolves that Shadow recognized as his sister Gale and his brother Swift. There was no sign of their brother and sister, Goldie or Silva, who was the image of Silver. They had both perished the previous winter from starvation. And Old Two Toes, the faithful and patient baby-sitter who indulged the cubs even more than Silver, was not with them. Had he perished, shot by a hunter, or starved to death after some hunting injury?

The cubs began jumping up and down and became impatient when each of the approaching wolves paused at one of Shadow's scent posts in their path to investigate it and then mark it themselves. Shadow ran out first to greet them, but it was Storm who received most of his attention. Storm was his father, his superior whom Shadow loved and respected. He clearly displayed his feelings by actively greeting his father, bowing low and twisting his head up to lick the side of the older wolf's mouth, his tail held low, wagging furiously. Storm stood quite still, with his head and tail held high, displaying his status and at the same time accepting Shadow. He then seized Shadow's muzzle in his jaws and gave it repeated affectionate bites, growling and whining at the same time.

Shadow rolled over onto his back and allowed the others to sniff him all over. He didn't permit this for too long and was soon up and asserting his rank over the yearling male, Swift, who was a cocky young upstart.

The two females, Grayface and Gale, greeted him affectionately. When Silver joined the melee, she briefly greeted Storm, displaying her submission and affection toward him. But she reacted aggressively when the others tried to sniff her. She was clearly boss over Grayface and Gale. When these greetings were over, the reunited adults began to play and dance together, whining and humming as they skittered, rolled, hugged, and pranced on the sandbar.

The cubs, who had shyly hung back in awe of the intensity of the reunion, caught the spirit of the adults and, gaining confidence, came out of their cover in the willows. As soon as the wolves saw them, they raced over to the cubs, and their meeting was filled with joy, tenderness, and curiosity. Grayface even threw up some meat for the cubs, while they, in their gay abandon, were jumping up to kiss the faces of the adults and then flopping over onto one side so they could be sniffed and nuzzled.

The whole pack stayed together for over a week, during which time the cubs developed a close attachment to the newcomers. Gale, who was a gentle and playful young she-wolf, was especially popular with the cubs. The boys were impressed by Swift, who was always showing off his superior speed and agility during the long hours that they spent playing together.

Before the pack split up, they joined forces and killed a large cow moose. But on the way home from the kill, the festive spirit was short-lived. Crossing a wide river valley where there was little cover, the pack was surprised by a plane that suddenly came over a ridge and flew down the valley, zigzagging to drive the wolves into the open and keep them running downriver.

The cubs were confused by the sudden panic of the adults, who immediately scattered in search of cover. Dusky was the first cub to sense what was happening and was soon safely concealed in a thick clump of reeds and willows. As the plane dived, rifle shots rang out, but the hunter was too late to get in a good shot at the wolves and signaled his pilot to circle back and made another approach down the valley. Storm had seen all this before. He had watched his mother crumple after one of those loud explosions that made his ears ring for hours. He wondered why this was happening, and he remembered the plane landing and two men skinning his mother and taking her pelt. But they never returned to eat her carcass.

Blackie and Blondie had moved out into the open and

were in danger. Silver gave a low warning growl-bark, and they bolted for cover. A few seconds later the plane appeared, but seeing no wolves, the frustrated hunter flew off, knowing that his chances would be better in the winter. Unknowingly he had provided the cubs with an experience that would greatly help them in handling attacks from a plane in the future.

Their spirits lifted when they got home. Old Two Toes was there waiting for them, and the reunion was almost as intense as when the cubs and the main pack came together.

Old Two Toes used to be the alpha, or leader, wolf in his youth, but Storm had now taken his place at the head of the pack. Storm showed more affection toward Old Two Toes than he allowed himself with Shadow, and he did not seize the old master around the muzzle. Old Two Toes simply ignored it when Storm started to growl and so avoided any conflict. He walked over to Grayface, who was lying down to rest, and stood over her. She raised her head and licked and nuzzled his quarters, performing the affectionate ritual that friendly wolves do to each other, reminiscent of the way in which a mother will clean her own cubs.

That night the wolves sang to the moon, happy to be together again, and the cubs enthusiastically supported the songfest with their young soprano voices. From far off they heard another pack singing, and even farther away, like a faint echo, the mournful call of a lone wolf. There was a restless sense of anticipation in the pack, and the cubs felt this, not knowing that before long, life would be very different for them. Winter was coming, and with it countless hardships that would test the resources of each wolf and of their combined strength as a pack.

13

The Pack in Winter

THE CUBS WERE confused the next morning when Shadow, Silver, and Storm started moving off across the river. They did not normally take this route when they took the cubs hunting. Silver called them to follow, and obediently the cubs set out with the adults, wondering just what was in store for them. Old Two Toes, Swift, Gale, and Grayface went off downriver. They would travel in a great arc and meet up with the others later in the day. The pack was now adopting its winter pattern of breaking up into hunting search parties and then coming together later in the day or sometimes two or three days later. Those wolves with the cubs would patrol a smaller hunting area. They would sometimes be joined by the others, who covered a wider range and would bring the cub pack to any distant kill that they might make.

The first snow caused much excitement when the cubs awoke from their temporary shelter in a hollow on the open range. They thrust their noses up at the big soft flakes and were completely mystified when the flakes vanished on their black noses, leaving behind tiny beads of sweet, ice cold water. Blondie reared up on her hind legs, biting at the flakes, while Tundra and Blackie shoved their muzzles into the snow and ran around like snow plows. Dusky was disconcerted by the strange things falling from the sky, and it was some time before he caught the mood and joined in the fun with his siblings.

All at once a huge white form rose up from nowhere out of the ground. The cubs froze to the spot. Then the white monster shook itself and suddenly turned into Silver as she threw off the sticky soft snow that was clinging all over her thick winter coat.

The next few days were an important learning time for the cubs. Familiar clumps of trees, rocks, and hillocks in their territory changed as the snow began to build up. The cubs were afraid at first. With time they got their bearings and rapidly adapted to this sudden change in their familiar world.

Wolves have an acute ability to recognize even the slightest change in something familiar. An experienced trapper avoids disturbing a stone or a tree branch in setting his trap and always keeps the earth as undisturbed as possible. Even then he might unwittingly leave a clue for the observant wolf, such as his scent, a broken twig, or a patch of flattened grass where he rested or dropped his pack. He will even use deer musk to mask his own scent.

The cubs also learned to conserve their energy when traveling in deep snow by following single file behind the adults. By stepping into the path made by the leaders, they did not have to waste energy making their own path.

They learned to avoid the valleys where the snow was deep and instead traveled along the ridges and hilltops where the sparse hard-packed windblown snow made traveling easy. From such high vantage points it was also easier to spot prey and to chase them down- rather than uphill. Usually one or more of the wolves circled and lay in ambush some way down the mountainside. They traveled all the time, constantly working their hunting range for prey, a territory of more than 1,000 square miles. The cubs were strong and kept up with the pack well, although Old Two Toes found it harder and harder to maintain the pace.

High up in the mountains the cubs learned to hunt Dall sheep, one of the hardest animals to capture because of their great agility on the mountainsides. They tasted ptarmigan, which Swift was skilled at catching. Almost invisible against the white snow, these fluffy white birds startled and tantalized the cubs by flying up from under their noses and then landing nearby to become invisible again, their white forms blending completely with the snow.

Tundra proved himself one day by being the first cub to catch the biggest animal by himself so far. He was moving with the pack, fanning out across a slope of crisp deep snow, when right beneath his feet he flushed a snowshoe hare that was napping in the milky afternoon sunshine. As quick as a flash he snapped and caught the hare in mid-leap and killed it with one powerful shake of his head. He paraded with his trophy and allowed none of the cubs to share it until he had eaten all that he wanted. Then there was a free-for-all tug-of-war, and the cubs shared his prize.

14

The World
of Wolf and Man

THE SUN NEVER ROSE high into the sky and seemed always
on the horizon like a red orb, glowing with a cold, distant
fire that cast long shadows and gave the snow a velvet pur-
ple sheen. The northern lights, those fantastic dancing mul-
ticolored phantoms of the Arctic sky, provided an ethereal
background to the wolves' dreams and eternal wanderings.
Their nightly choruses seemed to symbolize not only the
unity of the pack, but also the oneness of all things in nature, from which the wolves are inseparable.

76

The land of the midnight sun was now in the tight grip of winter, and the cubs experienced for the first time the intense cold. They all had luxurious winter coats and thick tails to tuck around their noses to prevent frostbite on this most exposed part of their bodies. They would shelter from the blizzard behind rocks or in hollows in the snow, often huddling together to conserve one another's body warmth. The snow, too, provided a good insulation against the intense cold.

By the new year the cubs, now nine months old and almost fully grown, were coping well with the hardships of their first winter, thanks to the knowledge they acquired and the support they received from their adult companions. There had been a heavy snowfall for three days, and the wolves, not being able to hunt during the storm, were hungry and anxious to secure a kill. All the recent kills had been picked clean. The snow was deep and soft, and the going would be slow and tiring.

In a small hunting camp many miles away, a hunter had been waiting for this day. He had come up from a large East Coast city and was keen to get some trophies for his den. Although he loved and respected animals in his own way, a trophy on the wall made him feel good inside. It was the kind of status symbol he needed to show off to his friends. A wolf skin or caribou head on the wall gave him a sense of fulfillment and power.

His pilot-guide started the plane, and they took off, heading to the same range where the pilot had spotted the wolf family earlier during the summer.

Shadow took the lead this day, followed by Storm, then

Silver, and the five cubs. Old Two Toes, Grayface, Gale, and Swift had taken off in a different direction, to fan out into a small forest of spruce trees on the side of a mountain. They had no luck and joined up with the others around noon.

In single file they trekked across an open lake, where the windblown snow was a little easier to walk through. Shadow, with his jaws open and tongue lolling out, taking in great gulps of air, forged ahead, breaking a path for the others in the snow. They stopped to rest and nibble the snow to quench their thirst. Dusky first heard the plane and alerted the pack in good time by standing up suddenly and pricking his ears in the direction of the sound. The wolves were caught out in the open, and there was only one thing to do—to turn back along their path.

The pilot directed the plane in anticipation of the wolves' movements, so that his client would have an easy shot on their first approach. The first shot, aided by a skillful pilot and a high-powered telescope mounted on the rifle, struck the snow in front of Old Two Toes, who originally in the rear of the line, was now the leader. And he was slow. Realizing this perhaps, he broke out of the path and made his own way over the lake, heading for a distant finger of spruce trees on the edge of the lake.

Seeing this large wolf break the ranks, and thinking it the leader with a prize head and pelt, the hunter fired countless shots at the old wolf. The pilot signaled the hunter to shoot at Shadow or Storm, who were better "specimens." But too late, he struck Old Two Toes. Feeling the white heat tear into his side, he twisted and bit at the invisible enemy, and then again as it ripped into his shoulder. His life melted a red pool into the snow, and his eyes, looking at the far mountains, never closed, but seemed to empty themselves into the wilderness.

Before the pilot had circled back for another run at the wolves, they had made good headway, thanks to Old Two Toes, and one by one they disappeared into the cover of the forest along the edge of the lake. The hunter emptied a few rounds after the pack in frustrated fury, and then the plane landed on its skis, making a white arc of snow as it taxied toward the lifeless form that was once Old Two Toes. The hunter, seeing the skinny old body and ratty pelt of the old wolf who had given so much to the pack, cursed and kicked the still-warm corpse. If only he had got one of the others. He saw how worn the teeth were and how battered the ears were—even his head would be useless mounted as a savage snarling trophy. And so they departed, leaving Old Two Toes to the carrion eaters—foxes, ravens, wolverines, and even starving wolves. Old Two Toes' body would not be wasted but would return to the wilderness.

It was another three days before the pack was able to catch a caribou; the prey was small, and there was little food to go around the entire pack, so they split up again into two parties so as to cover a larger hunting range. They had better luck the next evening, both parties making kills quite close to each other.

When they joined up and began to sing, Shadow seized a bone and paraded with it around the entire pack, not letting the others come near him. It was a magnificent display, his sleek dark body prancing over the snow with tail

held high in the air and all the hair along his back and tail bristling. He seemed to dare the others to challenge him; then abruptly he stopped, letting the bone fall in front of the others, who immediately ran over to investigate the gift but soon ignored it because they had been so well fed that evening. Shadow was performing the ritual of symbolic giving to the pack, using a token object, the bone, to express his status over the others, but also his role as the major provider. He was now leader, and Storm assumed second rank without a ritualized fight, which was not uncommon in wolves vying for top rank. They did not fight because they had a close bond of friendship, and recently, whenever Shadow did stare and even growl at Storm, he would avoid looking at Shadow and so avoid any conflict. Storm, a wise wolf, simply had passed on his responsibilities to his son after five years as leader.

Slithering and sliding down a snow-glazed incline one morning, the cubs were alerted by two little snowballs of fur scurrying across the hill in the opposite direction. Confused by what seemed from a distance to be snowshoe hares, but which smelled a little like Rastus, the red fox, the cubs took after the mysterious forms. Seeing the wolves after them, the two fox cubs, knowing the hillside well, quickly found refuge beneath a pile of rocks. These were the first Arctic foxes that the cubs had seen. They were used to their smell, often encountering it along the trail and by their old kills which the foxes had picked clean. Excitedly the cubs sniffed and pawed at the foxes' refuge. Growls and clicks and screams suddenly came out of the hole, a torrent of sounds even more abusive than from Mr. Grumbly, the wolverine. Blackie and Blondie rolled in the fox odor near the hole where the foxes had marked, while Dusky, Dawn, and Tundra took off to join the main pack that was now crossing the valley below to go up a far mountain ridge into the far western limit of their territory. Blackie and Blondie soon gave up on the elusive foxes, and as soon as they left, the foxes popped their heads out and barked defiantly and confidently. No doubt they thought that it was their terrible threats that had driven the fearful wolves away from their hole.

Toward the end of January a tension, familiar only to the older wolves, developed in the pack. This was the mating urge which became more intense as the days passed. Squabbles increased in frequency and intensity between males and between females. Silver was growing more intolerant toward Gale, who was entering her first heat. Silver was the highest-ranking female, and Gale was constantly testing her and Grayface for a chance to elevate her rank. She redirected her aggression toward Blondie and less often to Dawn, who kept to herself. The female cubs were disconcerted by this change in behavior of their elders and spent more time together, often roaming some way off alone, in pairs, or with one or more of their brothers.

Shadow, as the executive leader, was preoccupied organizing hunts and keeping a constant eye on the pack in case any trouble started. If a squabble did flare up, he would often step in and stop things. He was especially attentive whenever Silver was threatened and would instantly step to her side and support her. In this way she was able to keep her status as alpha female.

Swift became quite attached to Silver, following her around and looking longingly at her. Silver either ignored him or gave him the occasional snap when he got too fresh. Shadow looked upon him with an air of disinterest, knowing that the young male was no rival and that Silver was only interested in him. Conflicts and rivalry between the males were not so frequent. Much of the peace and order was due to the stabilizing effect of Shadow's leadership. Whenever Swift was severely rebuffed by Silver, he would often vent his frustrations on Blackie or Tundra, especially when Shadow was not nearby to intervene. One day Tundra stood his ground and challenged Swift, and Swift backed down, fearing the younger wolf whom he could no longer scare with his halfhearted threats. Tundra, son of Shadow, was destined to become a great leader of wolves, and already his personality was maturing and revealing the exceptional qualities of a leader wolf.

15

Spring Comes;
the Cycle Continues

AROUND MID-FEBRUARY, probably because of the tensions associated with the breeding season, the pack broke up. Shadow, Silver, Gale, Tundra, Swift, and Blondie formed one group. The other group was composed of Storm, Gray-face, Dusky, Blackie, and Dawn. Silver, Gale and Grayface were now in the height of the breeding season. Shadow was constantly at Silver's side, gently grooming her, nibbling her face and ears. They would often run "hand in hand" with their sides touching and engage in the beautiful slow-motion bowing, leaping, and embracing ballet of courtship play. Shadow even brought her three ground squirrels that he had caught one evening and laid them at her feet, pushing them toward her with his nose and urging her to take them for herself. But that springtime they did not mate. If they had, Tundra, Gale, Swift, and Blondie would have helped feed and guard the cubs, making the task of parenthood much lighter for old Silver. What stopped them from mating is one of the mysteries of nature. Perhaps it was because their hunting range would not support a larger pack, and there would not be enough food year-round to maintain all the adults, as well as a litter of cubs.

In a few weeks the snow began to shrink imperceptibly as the sun climbed higher into the sky and each day stayed longer and longer above the mountains. Slowly the earth began to breathe as the ice and snow melted into it. The ever-warmer seepage of water soon turned the rivers into torrents under great slabs of ice that eventually gave way and were carried off in the spring flood. The wolves now had to be more cautious crossing lakes and rivers. The younger ones soon acquired the skills of Shadow and Storm in testing the ice and recognizing dangerous surfaces of both snow and ice that might suddenly give way under their weight.

Occasionally during the short spring and summer months the two groups met and stayed together for a short while, but they would not normally come together on a more permanent basis until the following winter. With the first heavy fall of snow in midfall, the clear still air was again torn by the sound of airplane engines. Not one this time, but a trio of Piper Cubs. In one of the planes was the hunter who killed Old Two Toes, and he and his companions were now bent on bagging as many wolves as they could. The day was ideal for them, clear, no wind, and new snow that would make the wolves' tracks easy to spot.

Storm was leading his pack across an open lake in search of caribou in the foothills of the mountain range on the far side. The snow was deep and soft, and they were making slow progress. Dusky, Blackie, and Dawn were tired, and Grayface had injured a leg in an unsuccessful

encounter with a moose a few days earlier. One of the planes spotted the pack and homed in on them, radioing to the others where to come. In terror and confusion, helpless in the deep snow, and without cover, the wolves floundered while the planes alternately circled and dived upon them. One by one the wolves were destroyed. In a short time the air was silent again over the great white lake, scarred with blood and bodies of five wolves. The snow would soon fall again, and the wolves would be buried and forgotten. The sportsmen hadn't even bothered to take the wolves' pelts. This time they were simply out for the enjoyment of the kill. One, a rancher from the West, felt that the wolves were evil killers, and another, an Alaskan real estate agent, thought he was helping the caribou. That night they celebrated, proud that not one had got away. But one man remembered the large leader wolf that he had missed the previous year. He would soon be searching for Shadow.

The next day a well-known conservationist and a wildlife biologist employed by the state were flying over the range when they spotted the bloody scar that stood out like a red fan on the soft white skin of the lake. After circling twice, they gingerly tried to land, knowing that the lake might not be sufficiently frozen to support the weight of their plane. The skis of the plane cut smoothly into the snow, but the ice beneath began to give. Ready for this emergency, the pilot pulled the stick back, and they took off, unable to land. The men wanted evidence, and they needed photographs to show this slaughter to the world. They made several low passes over the sad remains of the pack, taking photographs, and then they left. They were too late to save these wolves, but perhaps they and their friends might be able to save others.

Shadow and his pack spent several days working in the tree-covered foothills and had good cover from the aerial hunters. Although the hunters scoured the countryside for Shadow and his pack, and although they sometimes spotted the pack's trail, they never saw another wolf. Returning home, they told other hunters there were still plenty of wolves in that vicinity for the taking.

Some of the photographs that the conservationist had taken turned out well. They were reproduced by a national magazine and within a week, the whole country knew of the murder of Storm's pack. Shortly thereafter, the wildlife biologist began a nationwide lecture tour to tell people about the wolves' plight. He told them that wolves are good animals, affectionate among themselves, and intelligent. He explained how they care for their young and how the caribou and other animals benefit from their relationship with the wolf. The fight to save the wolf had begun.

Within a few months, the wolf cause won its first victory: all hunting by air was banned by the President. But in Alaska, poachers continued to search for wolves, knowing that the penalty would be light. Also, the chances of being caught were slim because the wilderness was too vast to be effectively patrolled. But the number of aerial hunters was less, and Shadow and his pack were safer now.

Moving with the changing seasons, the wolves began to prosper and multiply. As the young matured, so the older ones faded away, to be replaced by new litters of cubs. Four years later Tundra became leader of a pack of twelve wolves, and he also became a father.

The last time Tundra looked out across the mountains and saw his family sunning and playing and the healthier herds of caribou migrating through the valley below, he was at peace.

A small boy, camping out on the range with his father

and little sister, heard the departing howl of Tundra echoing across the mountains. His father told him that it was a wolf. But the boy learned more. His sense of wonder gave way to a feeling of oneness, although he could not put it into words. The feeling remained. One day he would be able to tell his sister and his children.

For reasons unknown to the wolves, over the six years that Tundra was leader, there was more food each year, and life became easier for them. It was not only the skilled leadership of Tundra, but also the fact that caribou were more plentiful. It took the wolves a long time to get used to airplanes that no longer shot at them, and before Tundra died quietly one day from old age, the pack had increased to more than twenty. The wolves, the caribou and the wilderness had healed and were coming back into full bloom since man realized, almost too late, that he had to protect them by simply letting them be.

Author's Note

Slowly people have begun to realize that wolves are worth protecting. Even more important, they have begun to understand that the whole wilderness, of which wolves are one part, is worth conserving. The wolf, now an endangered species, has become a symbol of all that is right and in harmony in nature. It is modern man who in his ignorance has been wrong and out of step with nature. Not the wolf.

At one time, wolves could be found throughout the United States, but just as the Indians were driven off their lands and exterminated by new white settlers, so were wolves and other animals. The few remaining and impoverished Indian tribes were given reservations. The rich land that was theirs, land that they shared with the wolf and the mountain lion, was taken away. The wolf and the mountain lion were simply killed or forced to move to remote wilderness areas safe from man.

Increase of population and a growing country have, of course, meant that all wilderness areas could not be left intact as they were when the settlers first arrived. Modern man by necessity had to spread out and settle, but he went at it too fast and without the careful planning needed to avoid some of the terrible mistakes that have been made. Almost too late, he is desperately trying to put things right.

Conservation work to save wildlife and the wilderness involves real understanding and the means and ability to pass this understanding on to the public, to inform people about nature and to help them unlearn the myths and mistruths that have been spread through generations of a man-oriented society. It entails more than the fund-raising and political pressures that are also important.

The campaign to protect the wolf is to outlaw all hunting of any wild animals from the air, to stop the cruel use of steel traps and poisoned bait that cause slow and horrible deaths. More wildlife sanctuaries must be set aside, especially in Alaska and Minnesota, where wolves still live and have a chance to survive. In Minnesota those in the Superior National Forest are protected, while others outside the forest can be shot, trapped, or poisoned, but at least not hunted by air. In Alaska, although aerial hunting is illegal, it continues under the guise of management and control, and wolves are shot or trapped anywhere, at any time of the year.

In other sanctuaries and national parks, some of the larger predators such as the wolf and mountain lion should be reintroduced. Wolves once flourished in Yellowstone, and they have a right to be there now. It is not just that animals, like people, have a right to live, but that without animals, there would be no humanity. A New York cab-driver once remarked to me, "The less people care about animals and nature, the less they care about themselves."

To see a deer or a wolf or any animal in the world, instead of seeing it pacing in the confines of a zoo, is a unique experience—both fascinating and magnetic. To watch a wolf run free, living naturally in the wilderness brings one to an understanding of the beauty of nature and any animal's right to freedom.

Men who go to the wilderness to hunt and kill for sport refuse to understand and respect the natural world. These men hear the howl of the wolf and are afraid or hear it as a challenge. They see him as an enemy, as something to con-quer.

Other men return to the wilderness and respond to the magic of the northern lights, or the mystery of the migrating duck or salmon following invisible ancestral paths, or the howl of a wolf, or the silent darkness of the mountains. They begin to understand that man is only one small part of a vast universe made up of many forms of life. Only in balance and harmony can life continue to exist.

When you see a man wearing the fur of a wild animal, remember Old Two Toes, Shadow, Storm, Tundra, and the

94

others. When you become excited at the thought of going hunting, remember the men in the planes, chasing the wolves. When you hear a wolf howl when you are in the wilderness, rejoice. It may be the grandson of Tundra.

If we all begin to understand and to act, later generations will be able to share our experience of knowing an animal running free, and not just have a sad reminder in a museum of a stuffed wolf labeled "extinct."

Dr. Michael Fox
St. Louis, Missouri

About the Author

DR. MICHAEL FOX gets much of his information about wolves from firsthand observation. He has personally raised timber wolves, coyotes, and jackals, as well as red, gray, and arctic foxes. Dr. Fox is a noted authority on animal behavior, combining the background of a degree from London's Royal Veterinary School and a PhD in psychology from London University with a profound concern for the well-being and conservation of wildlife.

Dr. Fox is an associate professor of psychology at Washington University. He has written several books on animal behavior including *Behavior of Wolves, Dogs & Related Canids*, and *Understanding Your Dog*. The author's proceeds from *The Wolf* will go to further wolf research and conservation efforts.

Dr. Fox, his wife, Bonnie, and two children, Wylie and Camilla, make their home in St. Louis, Missouri.

About the Artist

As a young boy CHARLES FRACÉ began observing, collecting, sketching, and photographing the wildlife near his home in the Bear Mountain region of Pennsylvania.

His beautifully realistic paintings have been featured in nature books and magazines, and he has done many paintings for the National Wildlife Federation, including the 1967 and 1971 Christmas stamps.

Mr. Fracé, his wife, and two children, live in rural Mattituck, Long Island, where his large studio overlooks a marsh filled with birds and other wildlife.